CARLA'S FAMOUS TRAVELING FEATHER AND FUR SHOW

Written & illustrated
by

Barry Downard

MILK & COOKIES PRESS ™

Distributed by Publishers Group West

Carla's Famous Traveling Feather and Fur Show
Concept, story & illustrations
copyright © 2006 by Barry Downard

A publication of Milk & Cookies Press,
a division of ibooks, inc.

Distributed by Publishers Group West
1700 Fourth Street, Berkeley, CA 94710

This book is a work of fiction.
Any resemblance to actual events
or locales or persons, living or dead,
is entirely coincidental.

Design and art direction by Barry Downard.

No animals were hurt in the making of these images;
in fact they all had a real good time.-B.D.

ibooks, inc.
24 West 25th Street
New York, NY 10010

ISBN: 1-59687-171-7
First ibooks, inc. printing: April 2006
10 9 8 7 6 5 4 3 2 1

Editor - Dinah Dunn
Associate Editor - Robin Bader

Library of Congress
Cataloguing-in-Publications Data available

Manufactured in China

This book is dedicated to "animalfriends" everywhere.

Love

Respect

Care

Puk, puk, helloooo...
I'm Carla Chicken,
and this is my story.

From the moment I hatched,
my parents knew I was
going to be different.

Puk-a-Whoaa!!!!

Everyone told me,

"Scratch & roost,
scratch & roost,"

but I knew there was more to
being a chicken
than just scratching in the dirt.
I had an eye for STYLE...

Puk, puk, fabuuulous!!

I was a bit of a show-off
really...
always wanting to be
center stage.

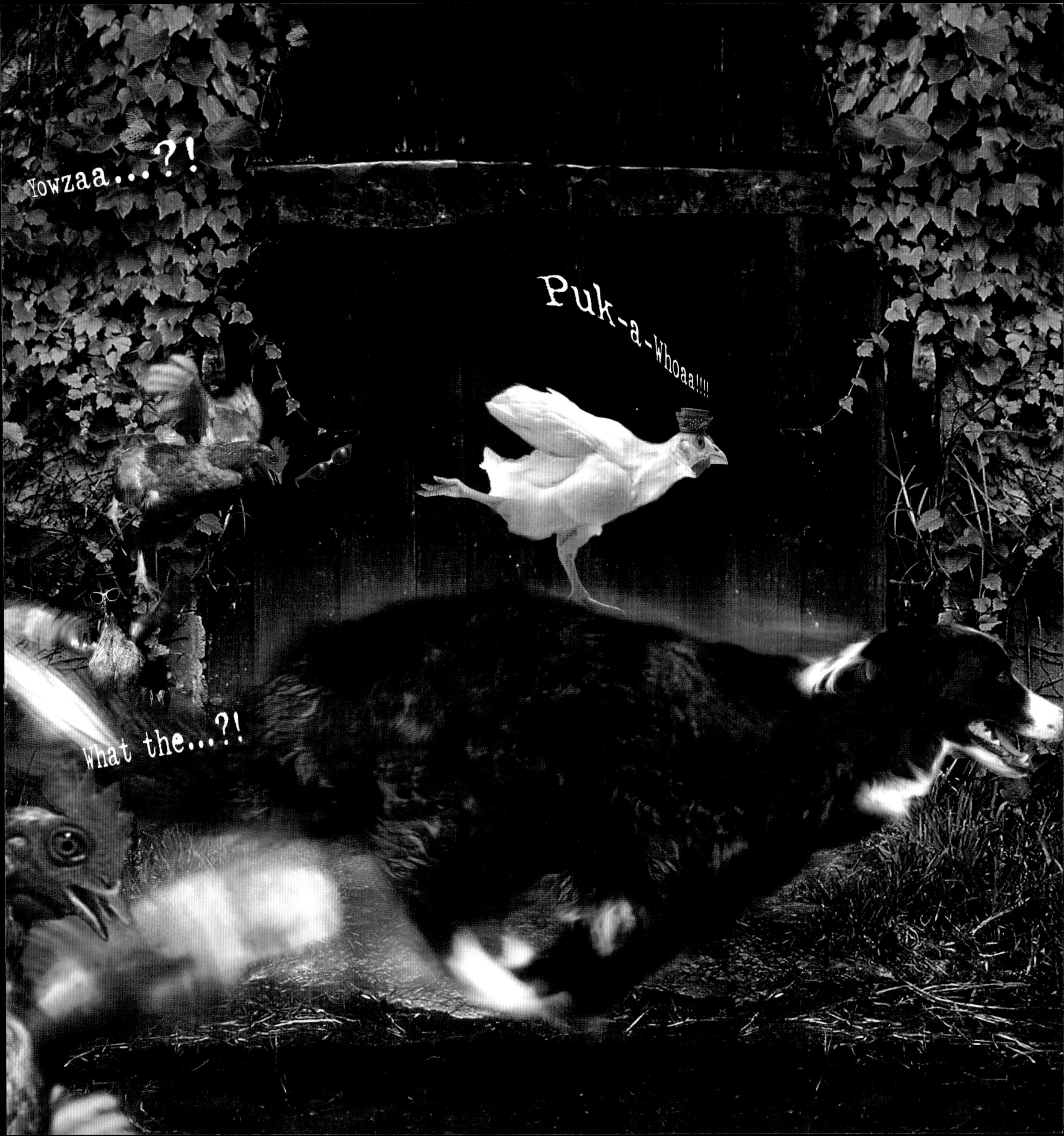
Yowzaa...?!
Puk-a-Whoaa!!!!
What the...?!

My teacher complained
that I didn't pay enough
attention in class.

But I was no dumb cluck.

Ordinary chicken life bored me.

I was always dreaming
about being something different,
exciting or glamorous,
and whatever I did
I knew was going to be
Famous!

One good thing about
all my daydreaming
was that it kept me
way too busy
to hang out
with those mischievous
Scratch
Soul
Sisters.

Hooo boy!,
They were just plain trouble...
tearing around the barnyard
on their scooter,
scaring the chicks,
kicking dirt into nests,
and worse!

Sheriff Barns
had only two words to say
about them...

Then one day it happened,
the most important day
of my life.

The ballet came to town! Yaaayyy!!!

While the Scratch Soul
Sisters were hatching a plan
to peck some pockets
at the show,
I began to dream
about what it would be like
to be in the spotlight!

Peck...Peck..

Peck...

Yo

Coming Soon
one day

Tchaicockski's

CHICKEN LAKE

Featuring

Margot Fonthen & Rooster Nureyev
and
The Royal Pullet Ballet Company

The show started
and the feathers flew!

The lights, the music, the cheers!

I knew then
that I had to be in
show business!

At last,
I could see my destiny.
With a little bit of
free-range imagination and a lot
of perspiration,
I set about
creating my own show.
I scoured around the farm
for the best talent
I could find.

I'm The GREAT CO

We're The Fabulous Pigelli Gi

CARLA'S FAMOUS TRAVELING
FEATHER AND FUR SHOW

Featuring:
CAIRO CHICKEN • ELVIS COW • THE GREAT COWZINI • FARAH FAUCET, THE TAP D...
FAMOUS TESS • OBI WON HENOBI • THE FABULOUS PIGELLI GIRLS • AND MUCH, M...

And I'm EGGS BENEDICT !

CARLA'S

.... We planned our first show
for my very own barnyard.

The Scratch Soul Sisters
wanted to do a scooter stunt
in my show,
but I was too busy planning
to **even** notice them.
That *really* ruffled
their feathers.

They **vowed** to bring me down
a
peg
or
two.

As I was getting ready for
opening night,
the Scratch Soul Sisters
decided it was their
chance to get even
with me for ignoring them.

They got into a huddle
to figure out a way
to scramble my plans.

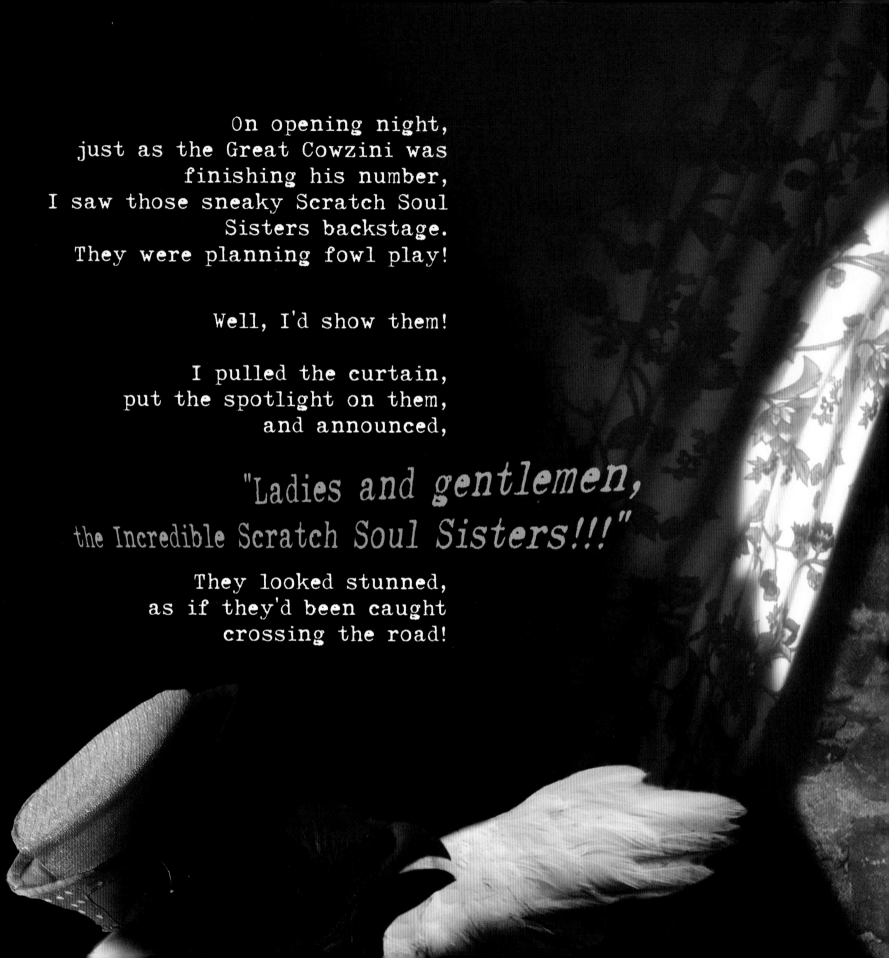

On opening night,
just as the Great Cowzini was
finishing his number,
I saw those sneaky Scratch Soul
Sisters backstage.
They were planning fowl play!

Well, I'd show them!

I pulled the curtain,
put the spotlight on them,
and announced,

"Ladies and gentlemen,
the Incredible Scratch Soul Sisters!!!"

They looked stunned,
as if they'd been caught
crossing the road!

Startled, they jumped
onto Cowzini's back
to do a balancing act.

"Yo, Ta-Daaah!"

As quick as a flash,
I launched myself
into a somersault,
spun through the air,
and landed
on top of them all!
Quite brilliant;-)

The crowd
clucked,

crowed,

oinked,

squeaked,

moo-ed,

bleated

and

squealed

with delight!

Everyone thought the trick
had been planned.
I was a star!

And that is how my
Traveling Feather & Fur Show,
(featuring the scheming Scratch Soul Sisters)
became a smash hit.

Look out for us
at a barnyard near you!

Let's get this show on the road!